DUMPED

Dee Phillips

RDZONE

READZONE BOOKS

First published in this edition 2013

ReadZone Books Limited
50 Godfrey Avenue
Twickenham
TW2 7PF
UK

The right of the Author to be identified as the Author of this work has been asserted by the Author in accordance with the Copyright, Designs and Patents Act 1988

Every attempt has been made by the Publisher to secure appropriate permissions for material reproduced in this book. If there has been any oversight we will be happy to rectify the situation in future editions or reprints. Written submissions should be made to the Publishers.

British Library Cataloguing in Publication Data (CIP) is available for this title.

ISBN 9781783220496

Printed in Malta by Melita Press

Developed and Created by Ruby Tuesday Books Ltd
Project Director – Ruth Owen
Consultant – Lorraine Petersen

Images courtesy of Shutterstock

ACKNOWLEDGEMENTS

With thanks to Lorraine Petersen, Chief Executive of NASEN, for her help in the development and creation of these books

Visit our website: www.readzonebooks.com

I have to talk to Chris.
I have to talk to him tonight.
But I don't know what to say to him.
Tonight, I have to make a choice.

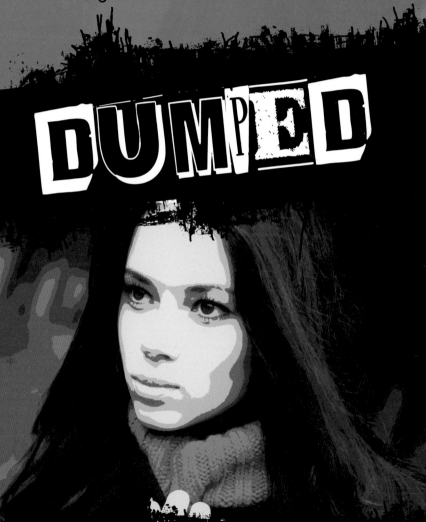

DUMPED

ONE MOMENT CAN CHANGE YOUR LIFE FOREVER

It's very cold tonight.
My feet are cold.
My hands are cold.
I'm waiting in the park.
I'm waiting for Chris.

4

COME ON, CHRIS. WHERE ARE YOU?

I jump up and down.
It's so cold.
Where are you, Chris?

Why do you always have to
be late?

Where r u Chris?

I have to talk to Chris.
I have to talk to him tonight.

But I don't know what to say to him.
Tonight, I have to make a choice.

Chris is my boyfriend.
We've been going out for three years.
I love Chris.
But does he love me?

I need to know because I have
to make a choice.

This is my choice.
Stay in London with Chris.

Or start a new life in Australia.

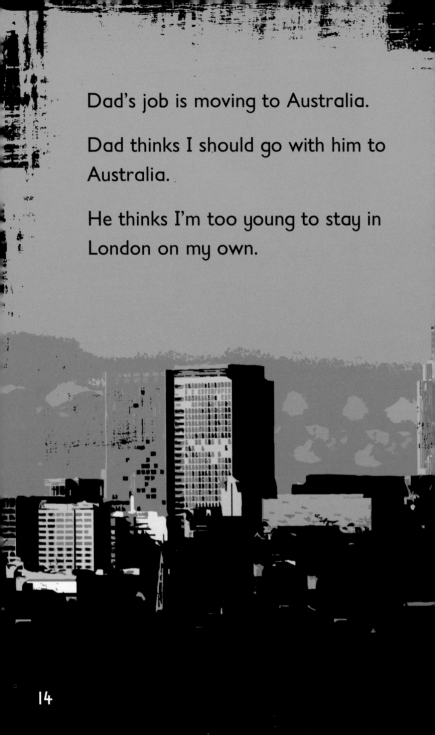

Dad's job is moving to Australia.

Dad thinks I should go with him to Australia.

He thinks I'm too young to stay in London on my own.

Dad says, "Life will be better in Australia, Vicky."

Becky is my best friend.
Becky thinks life will be better in Australia, too.
Becky says, "You are SO lucky, Vicky."
She made a list.

London

rain
white skin
college
work
Chris

Australia

sun
suntan
beach
beach parties
fit surfers

Becky says, "Go to Australia.
Tell Chris he is SO dumped."

I MADE ANOTHER LIST.

So that's why I'm waiting.
Waiting for Chris in the cold park.

Do you love me, Chris?
I need to know.
Because sometimes it's hard to tell.

Dad says, "That boy is a waste of space!"

Becky says, "Chris acts like your brother, not your boyfriend."

I say, "Do you love me, Chris?"
Chris just gives me his funny smile.

Chris sent me a Valentine's card.
Once.

To Vicky

from Chris

x

I jump up and down.
It's so cold.
Where are you, Chris?

Chris is always late.

Dad says, "That boy needs to get his act together."

Becky says, "That guy has NO respect for you."

All I do is wait — all the time.
Last week I was waiting outside the movies.
Tonight, I'm waiting for Chris in the cold park.

A new life in Australia.

Dad says, "Forget about Chris.
Life will be better in Australia."

Becky says, "Forget about Chris.
Think about all those fit surfers."

I jump up and down.
My feet are cold.
My hands are cold.
Chris is thirty minutes late.

No new messages

Where are you, Chris?

Dad is right. Becky is right.
I've made my choice.
I'm going to Australia.

No more cold.
No more waiting.
Tonight, Chris is dumped!

I feel good that I've made a choice.
But I feel sad, too.
I will miss Chris a lot.

But will he miss me?

Here he comes.
He looks cold.
He looks happy.
I feel cold.
Cold and sad.

But life will be better in Australia.
I will find a new guy in Australia.
A new guy who loves me.

Chris stands in front of me.
He looks down at me.
He holds out his hand.
There's a key in his hand.
Chris says, "I'm sorry I'm late. I had to pick this key up for you."

He says, "It's a key for our house.
Mum says you can stay with us."

Chris smiles his funny smile.

"Don't go," he says.

"Please stay."

DUMPED - WHAT'S NEXT?

Vicky makes lists to help her make a choice.
What choice might you have to make? For example:

- Going to see a band you don't like but all your friends do.
- Sticking up for somebody who is being bullied.
- Buying something expensive but that you really want.

  List the reasons for and against your choice.

COFFEE BREAK
WITH A PARTNER

Role-play two of the characters meeting for coffee the next day. Choose from Dad, Chris, Becky or Vicky. Think about the conversation they would have:

- What would they discuss?
- How would they feel?
- What advice would be given?
- How would that advice be taken?

LET'S TALK
IN A GROUP

What do you think Vicky should do? In your group, discuss what you would do in her situation. You could think about some of these questions:

- Is Vicky too young to stay in London on her own?
- Is she too young to settle down?
- Should she finish her college course? Or would she learn more by going to Australia?
- Does Chris really love Vicky?

THE COLOUR RED
ON YOUR OWN / WITH A PARTNER / IN A GROUP

Look at how the colour red is used in the book's design. What does red make you think of? Love, anger, lips, blood, roses…

Make up sentences beginning with 'Red is...'

- Organise your sentences to create a poem.
- Make a performance of your poem.

The colour red

Red is the anger I feel when people put me down.

IF YOU ENJOYED
THIS BOOK,
TRY THESE OTHER
RiGHT NOW!
BOOKS.

Sophie hates this new town.
She misses her friends.
There's nowhere to skate!

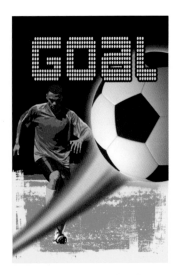

Today is Carl's trial with
City. There's just one place
up for grabs. But today,
everything is going wrong!

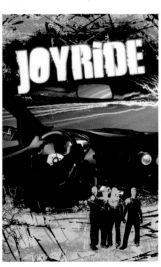

Dan sees the red car.
The keys are inside. Dan
says to Andy, Sam and Jess,
"Want to go for a drive?"

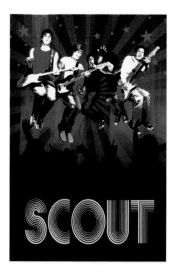

It's Saturday night.
Two angry guys. Two knives.
There's going to be a fight.

Tonight is the band's big chance. Tonight, a record company scout is at their gig!

Ed's platoon is under attack. Another soldier is in danger. Ed must risk his own life to save him.

It's just an old, empty house. Lauren must spend the night inside. Just Lauren and the ghost...